Dear Parent:

Am I Beautiful? is one of my favorite new books. The author, Else Minarik, is the author of the famous Little Bear series. With Yossi Abolafia's charming illustrations, this is a story to win your and your child's heart.

A native of Denmark, Ms. Minarik has said, "I consider the American language one of the most vigorous and colorful to be found on this planet...even in its simplest form, the form I use in my reader-picture books for children."

Make story time special in your home. It is a time when your child receives your undivided attention. Sitting in your lap or at your side, your child is building warm memories to last a lifetime. If your child spends time with a sitter or at day care, request that story time be included in your child's activities.

Enjoy!

Sincerely,

Fritz J. Luecke

Fritz J. Luecke
Editorial Director
Weekly Reader Book Club

Weekly Reader Children's Book Club Presents

Am I Beautiful?

BY

Else Holmelund Minarik

PICTURES BY

Yossi Abolafia

Greenwillow Books  New York

This book is a presentation of Newfield Publications, Inc.
Newfield Publications offers book clubs for children
from preschool through high school. For further
information write to: **Newfield Publications, Inc.,**
4343 Equity Drive, Columbus, Ohio 43228.

Published by arrangement with Greenwillow Books,
a division of William Morrow & Company, Inc.
Newfield Publications is a federally registered trademark
of Newfield Publications, Inc.
Weekly Reader is a federally registered trademark
of Weekly Reader Corporation.
Printed in the United States of America.

Watercolor paints and a black pen were used for
the full-color art.
The text type is Cheltenham.

Library of Congress Cataloging-in-Publication Data
Minarik, Else Holmelund.
Am I beautiful?
by Else Holmelund Minarik;
pictures by Yossi Abolafia.
p.   cm.
Summary: Overhearing other animal and human mothers
call their children beautiful, Young Hippo tries
to find out if he is beautiful as well.
ISBN 0-688-09911-4
ISBN 0-688-09912-2 (lib. bdg.)
[1. Hippopotamus—Fiction. 2. Animals—Fiction.
3. Mother and child—Fiction. 4. Beauty, personal—Fiction.]
I. Abolafia, Yossi, ill. II. Title.
PZ7.M652Am 1992 [E]—dc20
91-32562 CIP AC

For my granddaughter Zuleika, with love

"What a very hot day," said
Mother Hippo. "I'll have a nice
wallow in this fine cool mud."

"And I'll have a nice little walkabout,"
said Young Hippo.

So off he went through the tall
yellow grass, trotting along
on his little round feet.

Before long he came to a rock,
and there he saw a mother lion
playing with her cubs.

"My own little darlings," she purred.
"My sweet, silky, cuddly little darlings.
  You are the most beautiful darlings in the
  whole wide world."
And she nibbled at their little round ears.

"Pardon me, ma'am," said Young Hippo,
"but am I beautiful, too?"
Mother Lion studied Young Hippo's
leathery shape.
"Oh—that's not for me to say, young fellow,"
she told him. "Now run along."

So Young Hippo trotted along, and
soon he came to a lagoon.
There he found a father heron
giving dancing lessons to his children.

"Spread your wings," he was saying.
"Lift your legs daintily.
Bend your pretty necks. There!
Well, if you aren't the most beautiful
little creatures I've ever seen!"

Young Hippo tried a few dance steps,
but he couldn't do much with his neck.
"Look at me," he called to the father
heron. "Am I beautiful, too?"

Father Heron considered Young Hippo.
"I just can't tell," he said. "You have
no feathers. Best trot along, young man,
and ask someone at home."

Young Hippo went trotting back to his
mother. And then, on the way, he came
to a thatched hut. There he saw a lady
playing with her baby.

"Ah-h-h," she crooned, as she lifted her baby
high in the air. "You are the dearest, fattest,
most beautiful little baby in the whole world."

And she kissed the baby's small
fat fingers, one after the other,
till he squealed with happiness.

Young Hippo wanted the lady to look at him.
So he tried to sit up, but he fell over on his
back. There he lay, his four little legs sticking
straight up in the air.

"Look at me," he called. "Am I beautiful, too?"

"Oh, you silly little piglet!" said the lady,
laughing. She laughed and laughed.
She just couldn't stop laughing.
"Hmph!" said Young Hippo, getting back
on his feet. "I'd best ask my own mother."

So he hurried home, and
there was his own mother,
very happy in the mud.

"Mother," he said, as he tried to stand
on his head. "Look at me. Am I beautiful?"
"Are you WHAT?" asked his mother.
"BEAUTIFUL!" shouted Young Hippo,
and he flopped over.

His mother laughed. She climbed out of
the mud and said, "Sugarplum, all hippos
are beautiful. And you are the most beautiful
of all, because you are mine!"

And she gave him one of
the world's biggest kisses.
It was a beautiful kiss.

"I love you, little Mother," said Young
Hippo. "This next headstand will be
a perfect one, just for you."